Praise for Storyshares

"One of the brightest innovators and game-changers in the education industry."
— Forbes

"Your success in applying research-validated practices to promote literacy serves as a valuable model for other organizations seeking to create evidence-based literacy programs."   — Library of Congress

"We need powerful social and educational innovation, and Storyshares is breaking new ground. The organization addresses critical problems facing our students and teachers. I am excited about the strategies it brings to the collective work of making sure every student has an equal chance in life."
— Teach For America

"It's the perfect idea. There's really nothing like this. I mean, wow, this will be a wonderful experience for young people."   — Andrea Davis Pinkney,
Executive Director, Scholastic

"Reading for meaning opens opportunities for a lifetime of learning. Providing emerging readers with engaging texts that are designed to offer both challenges and support for each individual will improve their lives for years to come. Storyshares is a wonderful start."   — David Rose, Co-founder of CAST & UDL

Resilient Hearts

Storyshares presents

ISBN 9798885977258

Storyshares
Storyshares, LLC
24 N. Bryn Mawr Avenue #340
Bryn Mawr, PA 19010-3304
www.storyshares.org

Inspiring reading with a new kind of book.

Asians Aren't All Good at Math copyright 2024 Shekina Oh
Interest Level: High School   **Grade Level Equivalent:** 4.4

Staring at the Stars copyright 2024 Tahlia Allen
Interest Level: High School   **Grade Level Equivalent:** 5.5

Hiding the Dragon copyright 2024 Joseph Legaspi
Interest Level: High School   **Grade Level Equivalent:** 2.0

Book design by Saskia Globig

Resilient Hearts
stories of teen strength

Storyshares

Contents

Asians Aren't All Good at Math

Shekinah Oh

1

Do Math

I tapped my pen on the desk. My eyes squinted at the word problems in front of me.

Math was easy back in second grade when teachers made us practice multiplication tables. When fifth grade came, the tables turned. Math became a nightmare.

"Oh," my mom says at the dinner table every night. "Have you heard of the IMO? The winners this year are Asian. You're Asian, so you should go there, too."

Yeah, right. My grades weren't good enough

for the IMO. It was the International Mathematical Olympiad, and qualifying for it was as impossible as going to Mars.

My stomach churned as I scribbled a star on the math problem. A star meant I had no idea how to answer it. It was a code my friend told me to use for questions that seemed unsolvable.

I opened my phone to call my friend, but Mom barged into the room before I could hit the button. She never asks permission.

"Nicole, why aren't you done with your homework yet?" she asked, tapping my textbook twice. "You're supposed to be faster. Look at the time. It's already dinner."

"No problem," I said. "I can finish my homework after dinner. It's no big deal."

"Nah, you'll just be calling your friends again," Mom said. She rolled her eyes.

It wasn't like I called my friends for fun. We talked every night so they could help me with my math homework. Of course, I couldn't say that. They weren't supposed to be the ones who were good at math.

I was.

Flip, flip, flip. My math teacher walked around the room, giving us our test papers. Sweat dripped from my palms as he handed me my test paper: thirty logarithmic problems.

"You have fifteen minutes," he said, setting the timer on the projector.

I had a staring contest with the test paper, unable to answer any questions.

Voices of my friends' math lessons came into my head. "Log both sides. Change to exponential form. You can do this. It's easy." Math was the opposite of easy.

"You haven't answered anything yet," my teacher said, pausing by my seat the same way my mother did. "Anyway, I'm sure you will get a good score on your test."

Two days later, the results came. I failed.

* * *

My friends and I sat on the soft grass, facing the town. Brown and yellow birds flew over us as we chatted about everything under the sun.

"I got my report card, did you?" Ethan asked, sipping his soda. He sighed after swallowing the drink.

"Duh," I said, pushing his shoulder and laughing. "We go to the same school!"

"How's your math grade?" he asked. "I got an A."

Suddenly, a pang of jealousy hit me. My hands

shook. I wished I could grab his report card and scribble my name on it. How could anyone get an A in math? Twelve hours of work couldn't bring my grade up to a B+.

"Yeah, it's good," I said, swallowing and crossing my arms. "My math teacher likes me a lot. He says I'm smart."

My math teacher called me stupid in front of my parents during the last parent-teacher conference. Mom and Dad grounded me for two weeks after the meeting.

"Oh, that's nice," Amelia said. "I got full marks in my advanced math classes. Ninety-eight in advanced algebra two and ninety-seven in advanced pre-calculus."

My heart almost stopped beating. For a moment, I wanted to mourn my existence. Dad had always wanted a child like her.

"Looks like someone's going to Ivy League," Ethan teased.

Everyone else laughed too hard. It was like they had just watched a stand-up comedy. Someone even rolled down the hill while giggling.

Me? I spent the rest of the time staring at the sky, wishing that those were my math grades, too.

✷ ✷ ✷

Dad and I shared the couch, putting our feet on the table. We sat like billionaires on a fancy beach vacation, munching sour cream popcorn from the mall. Our eyes were glued to the TV as it blasted the news.

"Once again, Asian countries top the PISA charts in math," a blonde woman caked in makeup said. She spoke to her colleagues like a robot, debating the PISA scores.

Those scores were like gold to my parents. It was the biggest test on earth. Everyone from every country took it. Then, parents and teachers compared their children's scores. If someone scored below average, it meant failure for the rest of their life.

Videos of East Asian children studying with twelve books on their desks played while the newscasters argued about Asians being good at math.

See?" Dad said, pointing at the other kids on TV. "They're studying all day. Doing math. Meanwhile, you spend your free time on the computer."

"But I'm writing, Dad," I said.

"Is that a real job? Does it make money?" he asked, stuffing popcorn into his mouth.

I tightened my lips, hiding my tears. "You may not consider it a 'real job,' but to me it is, and I treat it like one," I said.

I wanted to scream at Dad's face, but that couldn't happen. "Good" Asian children only have one choice in situations like these: obey. And right now, Dad was telling me to be better at math.

I had to do something—everything—for better grades.

2

More Math

I lifted my head while looking through my packed calendar, cramming sticky notes on each square. Every second of my next month had math: math tutor, math classes, and math practice.

"Great job," Dad said, clapping his hands from behind me. "You will be a very successful person when you grow up."

Successful. The word rang in my ears. It seemed like everyone waged war with each other to be successful. How important must it be? Stories of brothers killing each other for success played in my head.

"Asians are good at math. That's why they're successful. If you're good at math, then you will be successful," Dad said before leaving my room.

I was supposed to be happy, but sadness sunk inside me. How could I be Asian but not good at math? Was I a failure?

* * *

A strange email came into my inbox: I won a writing contest.

I closed my eyes, imagining Dad hugging me and talking about my potential.

Not possible. It's not math. I had to be good at math, not writing.

Is everything all right?" my new math teacher asked me.

I nodded before continuing my work. She smiled at me and then wrote a long equation on the board. My old teacher was in the other classroom.

We spent the rest of the class answering different questions—hard questions. The concepts were like rocket science. Nothing could stick in my brain. My head hurt like crazy after class, causing me to walk like a penguin.

But for the first time, I felt proud of myself. My friends huddled around me after class, begging me to do their math homework. Mom spammed the family chat with compliments and stickers, praising me for taking the course.

I didn't take just any math class. I took the hardest math class in school.

∗ ∗ ∗

My back hunched in the new leather chair Mom had gifted me during dinnertime. The math textbook's pages rustled as I flipped through its chapters. Every lesson fit with each other like a puzzle. Except I had no idea what the topics were.

I banged my head on the book, hoping the words would stick in my brain. It didn't work. Answering a question was like decoding a foreign language. Worse, I still had to do my friends' homework and give them perfect scores.

My stomach churned. I felt the urge to sob and write my feelings in my diary, but I had to study like everyone expected. So I bent my back more and worked 'til midnight.

The next day, my friends refused to talk to me. It meant more math.

∗ ∗ ∗

I had spent the past few weeks studying from dawn until dusk. My failing grades hung on the wall before me as a reminder to do better. Math textbooks from the library were scattered all over my desk. Reviewers flew around the room.

I stared at the questions until I started seeing double. My eyes got heavy and the math worksheet got blurrier by the second. "No, please," I yawned, throwing myself into a pile of books. Beep, beep! The clock struck midnight.

When would I ever be enough?

3

Too Much Math

"Oww..." I moaned.

Acid bubbled in my stomach, raging like a fierce thunderstorm. My body felt like it was ripping itself apart. I curled myself into a ball on my bed, praying for the storm to leave.

"Nicole, are you not going to school?" Mom asked, entering the room. She brought a metal tray with chicken noodle soup.

"I can't," I said, my voice screeching through the room. The hours of studying left me unable to lift a finger.

"I'm calling the doctor," Mom said with a frown.

Two hours later, we sat beside each other, squeezing ourselves into the tiny phone screen. The doctor laughed when he saw us.

"What happened, dear?" he asked. His marble teeth shone through the screen.

"My child is sick. She has a headache and stomachache, and no medicine seems to cure it," Mom told him.

"Well, how do you feel?" the doctor asked me.

"Dizzy," I said, swallowing my vomit. "My back hurts like stones are on it."

"What have you been doing in your free time?" the doctor asked. He sipped a cup of tea.

"I'm so proud of my dearest daughter," Mom said in her sweet voice. "She's been doing math all day."

"Math all day?" The doctor's face crumpled. "Look, I did that too. That's too much."

"You did?" My face perked up.

He nodded, telling me stories about his Asian childhood. They were just like mine! He talked about how his supportive parents couldn't protect him from stereotypes, and how his teachers expected too much from him because of his looks.

Tears flowed down my cheeks as he shared story after story. So my struggles were real, after all.

24

For the first time, I felt seen. All this time, I thought other Asians couldn't relate to me because they were good at math, like my friends.

I sighed a breath of relief. It felt like releasing a thousand stones from my back.

"Honey, it's OK," Mom said. She hugged me as the doctor told us what to do. "Everything is fine, and you're fine."

Why did she say that? Tears also streamed down her face as she nodded at everything the doctor said. Did she face this pressure too? Was it the first time she felt validated?

I smiled at her like never before. Imagine living forty years with those expectations.

"So," the doctor told me, "listen to yourself and cut down the math, understand?"

An idea popped into my head.

4

Just Enough Math

I faced my schedule once again, giving my parents a sly smile. "Rip," I yelled.

We tore down all the sticky notes. Colorful paper flew around the room like confetti. We giggled, throwing crumpled notes at each other.

"Hey," Mom said. "Throw it at Dad!"

"Don't listen to her," Dad said as we ran around my room.

He threw a pillow at me before I could throw sticky notes at him. After chasing each other, we fell to the ground and laughed more.

"I'm sorry," Dad said, teary-eyed. For some reason, Mom and Dad couldn't stop crying since the doctor's meeting. "It was our mistake."

"Your mistake?" I asked. I was picturing them hearing the same things I always heard since they were babies.

Other people's words came into my head as I imagined their young lives. "You're Asian? Can you do my math homework, please?" "You have to be good at math because you're Asian."

Mom tickled me, and the words poofed out of nowhere. Gone, all gone. That's where those words went.

* * *

I looked at my old friends sitting at the other lunch table, loudly talking about advanced classes. The old me would have made up a million lies about my grades and hard classes. Now, I shrugged and bit my tuna sandwich without caring.

"Hey, you're in the writing club, right?" a boy with cute lips and monolids asked. I nodded, and he sat in front of me. "I'm Jacob. Nice to meet you."

"Nice to meet you, too," I said, shaking his hand.

We spent the rest of lunch chatting about our writing projects and things that made me feel fulfilled. If I dared to talk about writing with my old friends, they would've reminded me about the other Asians with engineering degrees making six figures.

Jacob didn't do any of that, so I let him into my life. Besides, I would never be with people like my old friends anymore.

After all, there was more to life than living for others.

Author's Note

Other people are surprised when I tell them about my struggles in math. After all, I am half Chinese, and my dad is a software engineer. The "Asian math nerd" stereotype made my situation worse. It was everywhere, from PISA scores to fictional characters. Of course, Asians don't have to be math nerds, but my young mind didn't see that.

When I read about some Asian genius, I wondered what was wrong with me. My math grades were shaky, and I wasn't a calculator who could solve every problem on earth. The "brainiac" stereotype made me feel abnormal and unloved, even though that was far from the truth.

As the years passed, academic pressure built up in my life, adding to the higher expectations set on me because I was Asian. I found myself chasing impossible grades and studying for twelve hours to reach my goals. Although hard work and dedication are valuable, too much of them could make you sick — like what happened to me. My eyes became red from studying, and acid boiled in my stomach from the stress.

I am in the ninth grade and still learning to cope

with academic pressure. Often, I have to remind myself about my worth outside of fitting into a stereotype. It's hard when you go against the current, or in this case, myths and stereotypes.

Of course, there's nothing wrong with being good at math or studying for a test. The problem arises when we take it too far—like expecting children to get perfect scores in every exam, racial stereotyping, or any other unrealistic "ideal." These expectations burden young people, preventing them from learning and exploring who they are.

This story is a simplified (and toned-down) version of my past few months. My biggest wish is for people to be more open about academic and societal pressure, and I hope people can identify with this story.

Staring at the Stars

Tahlia Allen

1

The icy dew on the delicate morning grass tickles my bare legs. I take a seat and watch as the light twinkles, cracking through the remains of the night.

My house faces the east. I know this because I grew up watching the sunrise.

My mother would set me on her lap. She would tell me stories about the wonders of the sky in Australia.

That was when things were different. Easy.

A body grumbles as the beauty of the day meets his darkness. The light awakens him on our driveway.

"Where's your mother?" his voice croaks.

He only talks about Mum when he's drunk. Lately that's more often than not.

My mum passed two weeks ago.

Ever since it feels like the world has been spinning out of control. The only things I can count on to be normal are the sun, the moon, and the stars.

2

I slip my hands under the armpits of my intoxicated father.

Thankfully, he is slim. I can heave him up toward our door.

I reach for the handle. I'm desperate to escape the cold.

The door swings open just out of reach.

My seven-year-old little sister's teary eyes greet me. She glances at my father and her lip trembles.

Great.

I don't mean to seem annoyed but clearly, I do. I know because she stares blankly at the ground, blinking away tears.

I release my dad's body with a thump. The noise makes my sister jump. I'm tired and running out of empathy.

Using my pointer finger, I raise her shivering chin and meet her eyes. Despite her stubbornness, they're betraying her.

When we make eye contact, I don't have to say anything. Her tears spill.

I crouch down so she can bury her head in my shoulder.

My sixteen-year-old body threatens to crawl up into a ball. The ache in my heart splits a little bit more.

The school counselor warned me holding everything in could lead to an eruption.

But I don't have a choice.

3

My sister's eyes dry, and my shirt is soaked. I haul my father inside. I rush to the bathroom, choking back my own sorrow.

This is the only place I allow myself to break down. Two minutes. Then I pull myself together and get back to the open fire.

But the flames still burn me in my safe haven. I slide my back down the locked door of my bathroom.

The sobs rack through me, silently, like waves in the ocean. I take a couple deep breaths. I wipe my eyes and stare into the mirror.

I pull at my rough skin. There are dark circles swallowing my face. I stare into a reflection I don't recognize. A reflection I don't want to know.

The deep huffs from the neighboring room remind me of my duties. Like my firefighter father, I embrace the flames.

4

Walking with my sister to school is one of my favorite parts of the day. Comfortable silence washes through me.

I can hear the beat of my ratty shoes crunching against the gravel. These five minutes are my time to stop thinking.

My seconds of silence. It's always been like this since before my mum's accident.

This is the only thing that's stayed the same. It will stay the same no matter what.

When the sturdy shadows of the looming school fence appear, I put on my mask.

I prepare to answer the questions with, "Yeah, I'm doing all right. Miss my mum, though."

I have a long, weary appointment with the school counselor. I'm dreading it in my bones.

Exhaustion clogs my mind and my heart rages against my rib cage. I cling to my breath, struggling desperately to inhale.

5

I blurt out goodbye, but it comes out in a shaky whisper. I march away from my sister.

The school buildings loom over me, towering over the grounds. My eyes dart in every direction.

I stalk past the calls of my friends. I barely register my surroundings.

I can't do this anymore.

I need help.

6

The weight sets on my shoulders. I climb the mountains. My back curls, hunching me over. I'm reaching out hopelessly for help.

I feel everything go quiet. The world feels blurry and far away. I'm in my head. Stuck.

I'm still walking, but I'm heavy.

I am not me. I don't feel real.

A warmth curls around my shoulder. I turn to see Chalise, the counselor, staring at me. Her eyes are drowning in concern.

Just as quickly as it stopped, the world spins rapidly again.

Everything snaps back to the hushed pace. I realize I'm standing in front of the office glass doors.

I look around and meet confused gazes.

Chalise guides me into her office.

I sink into the couch, letting it envelop me. For the first time since my mum was holding me in her arms, I feel at peace.

My heart slows, my hands still, and I breathe in the cool air burning my lungs.

7

Charise's emerald eyes wait patiently. The corners of her mouth curl upward, inviting me to speak.

The words flow out of me involuntarily. I tell her about my mum. The sky and my love for it. My dad crumbling out of reach. My concerns for my sister.

I explain the tugs at my heart every time I fail the ones I love. The desperate need to protect them.

The overwhelming fear that every second is our last.

She just nods along. She doesn't say a word until I collapse empty. Weightless.

It's my turn to sit quietly.

She explains strategies to help me. She's going to contact child services. Me and my sister will stay together. My dad will get help and a psychiatric evaluation.

We will most likely return to his care. All of us safe and healing. I close my eyes as the tears escape.

"Lyla." Her voice warms me. "Everything is going to be okay. You're safe now."

And those words sound so unreal, like I've never heard them before.

That night, I'm lying in my aunt's bed, spooning my sister. I turn to stare out at the night and the evening glow and the stars. I feel my mother's arms around me. Caring for me.

I whisper, "I love you" to the brightest star. It is shining its love down on me.

My mum's presence is in the sky. Now and forever.

Hiding the Dragon

Joseph Legaspi

1

What I remember most about high school is Tristen. For a long time, she was all I remembered. But it was not for the reasons anyone ever expected. Not even me.

We actually met in 7th grade. She came to our school mid-year.

I'll never forget the instant the teacher brought her into our classroom.

Her green eyes struck me first. They added to the bright glow of her face. It was like a light from her went straight through me. I thought she really was an angel. She was just that beautiful.

Every day, I had trouble looking at her. I had to keep looking away or I knew I'd never be able to take my eyes off her.

Her outward beauty wasn't all that got my attention. She had this mystery around her.

I only knew she transferred from the school district of Brookfield, which was in a very wealthy neighborhood. But ours was not. Plus, it was made up of Hispanic and Asian kids. I was Filipino.

There was something else unique about her besides her eyes. She had porcelain skin and red hair.

I wanted to introduce myself and ask where exactly she lived, but I was too shy.

It turned out she was braver than me.

2

I saw her glancing at me now and then. I figured it was because of my background. I was the only Filipino in school, and I stood out. One day, she walked straight up to me and asked, "You're Juan, aren't you?"

I was so nervous that I couldn't speak. So I let her fill the silence. She introduced herself.

Then everything I couldn't say before came out in a rush.

"Tristen, do you know what? One day, I thought I saw you walking to school ahead of me. You were on the same road I was on. But I don't know. Maybe it wasn't you. It's a long walk."

"Oh? Where do you live?" she asked in an interested tone.

"Eleven Smith Street," I said.

"No way!" she exclaimed. "I live two blocks away! Twenty-two Smith Street!"

"That means we should walk to school together," I said playfully. Inside, I was wasn't even hoping that would ever happen.

"OK," she said with a wide smile.

I had to pinch myself. I couldn't ask her to repeat it. So I asked my classmates nearby if she really did say that or if I was dreaming. It was too bad, though. We had this conversation near the end of the school year.

But at the start of 8th grade, we picked up where we left off. We walked together each day.

3

To get to our school, we had to go through "the Clearing." It was a wide stretch of land with very few trees. The ones there were low enough to see the school from our homes, and our homes from the school.

In the Clearing, the sky spread out wider than it looked downtown or in the nearest city.

We walked through the Clearing every day until high school.

That's when she led me to the biggest decision of my young life. It would become a choice I never expected.

I would trade anything never to face that kind of decision again.

4

Our high school was further than middle school, but we still walked together.

She was tough. No matter the weather, she always stood tall and walked tall.

We walked in the heat. We'd be busy slapping mosquitoes on our necks and arms.

We walked in the cold. We'd sprint and huddle close to keep each other warm.

She loved to read and told me about every book she read. Her face and hands were so expressive. They were always moving with every word from her mouth.

Most of the time, we rested halfway at a tree stump, like it was there just for us. We'd just sit down and gaze at the bright, open sky.

We'd watch birds that flew up and never landed. It was like there was no limit to where they could go. We dreamed it would be the same for us.

"I'm going to be a professional artist," I said proudly.

"And Juan, I'm going to get all A's. I'll get into the best college and be somebody important. No one will ever ignore me again."

"Who's ignoring you?"

"Not you," she said, putting her hand softly on my shoulder.

We sat on the grass by the side of the road and stared up at the big sky. It was like it was staring back at us.

"Sometimes I see it all as a blank canvas," I said, searching the sky for words to describe my thoughts. "Just waiting for us to fill it up with..."

"With our wildest dreams, right?"

"And who knows?" I said with a shrug.

"Yeah," she added, shrugging back at me. "They might come true."

5

The first year of high school, we carried around so many books. In our second year, we carried double that load.

The first day was the hardest. Some of the books we could keep at home. The problem was getting them there.

Her dad was supposed to pick her up that first day. But he cancelled at the last minute.

She revealed that her mom was a lawyer. Her father was a stockbroker. They both had jobs where they could make a ton of money. But they also needed a ton of time to get their work done.

"They use 'family time,'" she said, with the saddest voice.

"Don't worry," I said, trying to cheer her up. "I got this, Tristen." But I almost dropped her bag the second I picked it up.

"Are you serious?" she scoffed. "You can carry mine and yours, too?"

"Yeah, no problem," I said with a grunt. Sweat was already pouring down my face.

"Yeah, right!" she laughed.

We walked for about five minutes when I stopped. I turned to her.

"Are you still... laughing at me?" I tried to say while breathing heavily from all the weight.

"Of course not!" she said, laughing again.

6

Though she covered her mouth all through the walk, I could tell she was smiling and giggling the whole time. I was glad she wasn't sad anymore, but this weight was really starting to hurt me.

"Stop!" I finally shouted with a laugh and in between breaths. "My arms and legs... already breaking. You keep making me laugh! Now my stomach hurts, too!"

It was useless. She just kept laughing.

If I had a mirror, I could see myself all drenched with sweat. My face was probably twisted in every embarrassing shape from the pain. That's what she must be laughing at.

We were barely halfway to her house when she stopped at our tree stump.

"OK, I think you've had enough!" she said with a sigh, stepping close to me and taking her bag off my shoulders.

I muttered something like "thank you." Yet I couldn't imagine anything coming out of my mouth except my heaving breaths and painful grunts.

She dropped the bag on the ground.

"You weren't kidding around. This is super heavy!" she said with a concerned tone. "You OK? You didn't sprain yourself or anything, did you?"

I waved her off. I spoke with my hands that I'd be fine.

For the next minute or so, she just stared at me. She was patiently waiting for me to catch my breath.

"Hey, Juan," she said, still standing close. "What would you do if I didn't stop?"

"I'd keep going," I replied after a big gulp of air.

"Really?" she said with a slight smile. "Why?"

7

"Tristen, come on," I answered, better at breathing now. "You think a guy as exhausted as me right now has any energy left to lie?"

She moved even closer. I could see my reflection in those eyes. They continued to stare at me. My guess was that she simply didn't believe me.

"I'll prove it. Let's go," I said, as I grunted and reached down for the strap of her bag.

Thankfully, she stopped me with her hand.

"But why?" she asked, her voice suddenly softening.

I gazed at her pretty face. I couldn't stop looking at her even if I had full strength.

Oh boy, she picked the perfect time to ask me a powerful question like this. As I had told her, I was too tired to hide or fake an answer. I had a feeling she'd keep asking until I gave in. So I did.

"For you, Tristen."

She stood there with no response at all.

My first reaction was that I screwed up, or at least my tongue did.

In my sudden nervousness, maybe I misspoke and said, "good morning" or something totally non-sensical.

To make sure I spoke with sense this time and complete clarity, I added, "I'd do anything for you."

At that, she held both my hands and kissed me. It was warm and gentle.

She turned me into someone else. I became like the wind. I could fly.

She took me somewhere else, too. Some part of me soared high. I flew way past the heavens. I don't think I ever came back down. There we stayed until the day touched night.

We ended up carving our names on that tree stump. Our names were still clear under the blue shade of twilight.

I thought that was the best day of my life.

Then life surprised us again.

8

She kept apologizing for making me carry all that weight. I told her she didn't have to do it so much.

To make it up to me, she used up all her allowance money to register us for a pottery class in town. I had suggested that maybe we could take it together one day.

I only mentioned it once and briefly during one of our walks. I was surprised she remembered.

We would learn to create different types of sculptures. It was in a gallery that used to be a warehouse.

We came an hour early. But a long line of people had already formed at the door.

I could tell she was as excited as me. She kept peeking into the foggy windows to see the paintings and ceramics inside.

"What do you see?" I asked.

She described pottery and paintings that decked the walls. They were spread out under a big chandelier made of clear wine bottles.

Once the class started, we followed the crowd. There was a sculpture made of fruit and flowers. It stood on folds of curled ribbons. They were all on a shiny white plate.

"So pretty," she said with a cheerful sigh. "I've never seen anything like this!"

What she saw through the windows was just the beginning. There was more pottery on long shelves and leaning against the walls.

One stood out as high as the door. On the far end was a wall of abstract art paintings. I stared long and deeply at them.

"What's wrong?" she asked.

"Nothing, why do you ask?"

"You look so serious. It's like you see something there that no one else can see."

"My parents say that a lot when I look at art. They say I have a gift. But I don't know. I guess I just see things others don't."

9

The instructor wore a red bandana and black jeans with paint smears on them. She began the lesson with these words:

"Working with clay is about perseverance. You need to keep working on it no matter how hard it gets. Keep your eyes and hands strong and steady.

"You may get tired or distracted. But stay with it. One flinch at the potter's wheel and you destroy it all. Clay can break apart with one stray act or one moment of doubt.

"Treat every ceramic figure with the same gentleness. In time, you'll be surprised how strong clay will get."

She held up a shiny but very thin plate. I thought a sneeze might crack it apart.

"This is thousands of years old," the teacher said. "Kids, isn't it amazing how clay survives the centuries! But how? It's so fragile! Maybe its only purpose is to go on, no matter how impossible it seems."

Tristen bought it and gave it to me.

I smiled. She smiled.

"Thanks," I said, "but you don't have to buy this for me."

"I want to thank you for this day," she said.

"Thank ME? It was YOU who thought of this awesome class!"

"I mean I want to thank you for being with me," she said, putting her hand on my arm. "I had a great time! I always do, everywhere we go."

"I don't know how to thank you," I said.

"I can't wait to see you up there," she said.

"When I'm up there as an artist, you'll know. It was because of you."

I would turn out to be right. But not the way I wanted. Things would soon change.

10

A few weeks later, I introduced her to both my parents. My home was so unlike hers. It was simpler.

We lived in a smaller house and even smaller backyard. We didn't own much furniture. Plus, the furniture we had wasn't the expensive kind.

My parents greeted her warmly at the door. They chatted with her for a bit, then Dad invited Tristen to bring her parents over for a cookout one day.

"My dad loves to grill," I said.

My mom said she was preparing some lemonade. We sat on the sofa while we waited.

"Your parents are so nice," she said. "I mean it. They're exactly as I expected from the way you talked about them. Really cool. They let you be who you want to be and do what you want to do."

She stressed again that her parents were mainly interested in money. All they talked about were three things: Work, money, and making more money.

Someday, they planned to move into a mansion in one of the richer towns.

"Wait, what?" I asked, nearly falling off the sofa. "Move? Are you serious?"

"Oh, Juan. Sorry for the bad news," she said, looking at me with trusting eyes. "I just want to be honest. I don't know when, though."

"Nearby?" I asked, sounding more like a request. Taking her hands in mine, I said, "Tristen, I'm begging! Please, tell me it'll be somewhere near!"

"Yeah, yeah, yeah." She said each word louder and louder. "We'll still be together."

"Promise?" I squeezed her hand tightly.

She let go of her right hand, stuck out her pinky and curved it like a little girl raising a teacup. "I promise."

She shook my pinky with hers. Then she sealed her pledge with a kiss.

We held each other for the longest time.

That was my doing. I didn't want to let go. I realized then and there that I couldn't stand the thought of losing her.

I wish I could say she put an end to my worries. I wish I could say that was the end of our story.

I wish I could say our feelings for each other were strong enough to face anything. But as terrifying as that news was, little did I know the worst was yet to come.

11

A month later, she started eating less and less. Her teeth and gums were bothering her.

She had to have her wisdom teeth removed. She kept holding it off as long as she could. Taking them out would hurt very much and take some time to recover.

The pain got worse and worse. After her 15th birthday, she had had enough and decided to get them out.

I often went with her to get pills for the pain from the drugstore.

This lasted for a few weeks, until she told me I didn't need to go with her.

I thought it meant she'd go with her mom or dad, but she went by herself. Though I was worried about that, I was more concerned with why she went so many times.

As soon as I found out, I said, "It feels like you need to go there a lot. Aren't those pills supposed to last for a month or so?"

"I just do what my doctor tells me," she said in a flat tone.

"Then are you sure you don't need me to go with you?"

"Nope, I'm good," she said, without looking at me.

"Why don't your folks take you?"

"It's none of your business, OK?"

That was the first time she snapped at me.

"Tristen, are you OK?"

"Fine. Sorry. I just have... a lot of homework. I didn't do so good on the practice SAT test. I need to do better."

12

Another day during lunch, I saw her grab some books from her bag and pill bottles fell out. The name was the same on each of them. But it was a long name. I couldn't pronounce it.

There were a lot of them.

"Do you need all of these?" I asked, staring at her bag.

"Yup. When I stop taking them, I feel sick, like throwing up."

"That doesn't sound right."

"Don't worry. My doctor said it was OK."

"How many do you take?"

"Enough," she simply said.

"Maybe you should double-check with another doctor," I suggested.

"I don't want to grumble about this with you or anyone else, OK? So let's drop it."

I'll never forget the way she said it. It was like she was talking to a stranger. Her tone wasn't as friendly as usual.

It was at this time that she started writing more and more poetry. She wrote one that was in the shape of a heart.

A special place
In my mind, set
Aside to hold memories
To come, of
Me
and
You.

She sent it to me to show she was fine. This was her way of saying she was sorry for being rude.

But as the days went by, her voice started getting weaker. Dark circles started appearing under her eyes.

My fears got so bad I went to our school counselor for advice.

13

Students usually went to Dr. Harmon if they had problems at home or were in fights or failing classes.

I had none of the above.

It felt weird for me to go to her. I really didn't want to go to her office, but I did it for Tristen.

She wore small glasses and had silver hair tied in a ponytail. Her office was small. We sat at an angle to each other, but so close I could shake her hand.

She spoke in a low voice. It was calm, but it only relaxed me a little. I was sweating more each minute and didn't know where to begin.

"I have this friend..." I began to explain to her. Then I stayed quiet for a long time. "I think my friend is sick. I mean... tired. I mean..."

"What do you mean by 'sick'?"

"I... I can't describe it."

"Hmmm. I see. Juan, please tell me more about your friend. Why are you so worried about him?"

"I don't know... I can't prove it. I just have this funny feeling he's not well."

"Can you give me more details?" she asked, writing something on her notepad. "What exactly is wrong with him?"

I didn't like the way she wrote down what I was saying.

"Dr. Harmon, can I come back another time?"

"Why? We just got started."

"I can't tell you any more."

"Why not?"

"I need to talk to him first."

"Can you ask him to come to me himself?"

"Well, he's... not the type to complain. I mean, shy. Okay, look, he doesn't even know I'm here talking about him."

"He sounds very afraid. Why?"

"Not afraid. She just doesn't think anything is wrong."

"She? I thought you had called your friend 'he.'"

"Umm... Yeah, no... I mean, I'm kinda confused about it all right now."

"I can see that, Juan." She put down her pen and said sternly, "If your friend isn't feeling well, you need to tell me who he or she is. Your friend may need a doctor right away."

"She's already seeing one. You know what? I think it's nothing. Thanks for listening."

I walked out of her office.

14

The next weekend, I saw Tristen reading *Dr. Jekyll and Mr. Hyde*. She would read it all the time.

I reminded her that our English teacher asked what our favorite books were one day, and she said hers was *Frankenstein*.

She was surprised I remembered. She was touched, but also seemed bothered by it.

"What is this thing with you and books on monsters?" I asked her during our walk to school.

She whispered in my ear. "Don't tell anyone. I'm writing this story about me and this dragon."

"Why so secret?"

"I can't tell you. I guess it's scary. It's even scaring me a lot."

"Wow. Can I read it?'

"It's not done yet."

"What's it about?"

"About a girl, and she's hiding this... this dragon... inside of her."

"Yeah, that does sound scary. How does it end?"

"I don't know."

Then a strange thing happened. Her eyes were full of tears.

She told me never to tell anyone that was her favorite book. It was hard keeping this secret.

I knew what the dragon meant.

It became even harder hiding my fears and worries about her. The more I pushed them away and fought them, the more they didn't go away.

Every day I would come home and fall asleep. I had to put an end to this. Yet I still didn't know how.

15

During our next walk, her school bag fell, and her pills spilled out. As I went to pick them up, she screamed at me as if I was touching her most prized possessions.

"Don't ever touch these!" she screamed.

It was suddenly awkward. We were silent throughout the rest of the walk.

At last, she broke the silence when we got to her home.

"Sorry for shouting at you. Promise me you'll never tell anyone about the pills."

"Tristen, is everything really OK?"

"Yeah, Oh I forgot to tell you the great news! I got a high score this time on the SAT practice test!"

I congratulated her. She also wrote another great poem that her English teacher loved.

"It's amazing what these pills can do!" she cried out.

"Wait, are you still taking them?" I asked her.

"Yeah, so what? I feel like I can do anything!"

"Tristen, you don't need pills to do those things. You're smart and talented without them."

"Why do you want to ruin my achievements?" she asked in an angry tone.

"I'm not," I tried to explain. "I just wonder why you're still taking them if you're already feeling better."

She moved very close to me and asked, "Did you tell anyone about these pills?"

"No, but I think they're making you sick."

"You're imagining things."

"Like the dragon you're hiding?"

She turned around and walked away.

I never saw her act like that. I felt like everything was falling apart.

16

I went to Dr. Harmon's office a few more times, only to turn around each time.

Finally, she caught me. She called me back and looked at me for the longest time. It was like she was trying to read something on my face. She then asked me to come inside.

"I have nothing to say," I told her.

"Maybe not, but please come inside anyway. I only need a few minutes of your time."

"I don't see the point."

"Well, I do. I have something important to tell you. It won't take long."

I paused to think about it. Then I agreed.

"Juan, I don't just want to say this. I need to say this. And you need to hear this." Dr. Harmon was direct and honest. "You may think you're hiding it well. But I see it in your face and eyes.

"They look strong, active, and intense. That's a lot of work for someone who has nothing to say. They're trying to scream something out loud even though your mouth is silent."

I nodded.

"I've been thinking about you quite often lately. I believe you know what to do. You just don't want to hurt anyone, especially yourself. But if you really care about your friend, you'll get her some professional help right away."

I nodded again.

"My gut feeling is that you care very much about your friend. Let me help. I'm always here. Please, Juan. Do it for her."

17

Over the next couple of days, Tristen started staying away from her friends.

On our next walk, I asked her again, "Are you really OK?" She shrugged this time.

I took her hand in mine.

"Your hand. What's going on?" I said, beginning to panic. "It feels so thin and weak."

"Just tired," she said feebly, then turned to me. "What?"

I gave her a grave look. "It feels like it's also trembling a bit."

"I'm nervous around you. I like you. A lot."

"Me too. But Tristen..."

"What?"

I paused. I didn't know how to say it.

"Something is wrong, isn't it? Don't play around with me anymore! Are you sick?"

She slid her hand quickly away from me as soon as I said this.

"What wrong with YOU? Can't you see? I'm fine. I'm walking, aren't I?

Out in the sunlight, she looked like the oldest 16-year-old in town. Her pale lips narrowed to form a weak smile.

She coughed many times along the way. Yet it didn't sound like the cough of a cold.

I also saw she wasn't walking straight. It was like her head was in another world.

As soon as we got to school, she went off to her class.

I, on the other hand, rushed to Dr. Harmon's office.

18

I sat down without saying hello.

"She's Tristen, my girlfriend." I went straight to the point. I drew in a deep breath and said with a break in my voice, "She keeps taking more and more of these pills. It's making her sick. Please help her."

"Thank you, Juan. I know this wasn't easy. You did right. We'll get her help."

As she left the room to get Tristen, I buried my face in my hands. I didn't cry, but I broke down inside.

I knew things would never be the same with us. It was just a matter of how much she would forgive me. That said, I didn't think she would.

Sadly, I was right.

She emailed later saying she was too angry to ever to talk to me again.

My parents will kill me! This goes on my record! I'll never get to Ivy League schools. I'll never even get a decent job! Are you that ignorant?

I replied, *I'm not ignorant! I realized that might happen. But I care about your life more.*

How could you do this to me? she wrote back. *I trusted you!*

Tristen, I love you. I didn't want to lose you.

I did too, but not anymore! she answered. *I never want to see you again!*

19

Tristen didn't speak to me for months. I stopped eating and sleeping well. My grades dropped. I went by her house many times, but her parents told me to go away.

I stayed forever at the tree stump where we carved our names. I thought about her day and night.

I finally went back to Dr. Harmon. This time, it was for me. She said something that gave me a little comfort, even if it wasn't that much.

"It's my fault," I told her.

"No, it's not," she said. "It's not Tristen's fault, either. She may come back. She may not. Sometimes, we just have to give up control and let go."

"I can't do that. I never felt so happy with someone. I never felt so down as I do now."

"Honestly, when you first came to me, I thought it was really you who had the problem," she said. "But I must say, I do see some of the same behavior patterns."

"What do you mean?" I asked her. "I don't have an addiction problem."

"Juan, you have to quit Tristen."

20

The months turned into a year and soon, I was graduating. Tristen did get help, but found another boyfriend.

I wasn't moving on. I was so numb from it all. I still couldn't even cry.

One day that summer, my dad heard me making noise in the garage. I was tossing out some junk into the garbage bin.

"What are you doing, son?"

"I don't need these drawings anymore. I'm not going to that art college."

He went to the garbage and took out paintings I made of her.

"I don't want anything to remind me of her," I said.

"I know. You want to dump it, that's up to you. But you painted that, not her." He punched me softly in the chest. "You faced it. Expressed it. That's art! That's why it's so important."

He gave it back to me. I took it and clutched it tightly to my heart.

"Son, I know you better than any man in this world. You're so young and you've been through so much."

He took my other drawings and put them back on the shelf.

He turned to me and looked me hard in the eyes. "Oh boy, I swear. You'll make a darn great artist."

As he walked me back inside the house, I caught sight of the thin ceramic plate on the far end of the shelf. I recalled that memorable day with Tristen.

"That's right," I said to myself, "the only purpose."

21

That night, I couldn't sleep again. I went to get a glass of milk when my mom heard me.

She brought me a picture of my pet rabbit. He died when I was about five years old. I cried so hard.

She said to me now like she said back then, "We have to say goodbye to those we love. Our grief will always be there and not there, like birds in and out of the clouds.

"Then one day, you'll wake up and out of no-where, you'll find..." she put her arm around me like she used to cradle me and continued, "it all went away."

I lay my head on her shoulder like I did back then. Her words, her voice, and the photo worked like a magic time machine. I was five years old again. My guard was down.

The dragons and monsters under the bed don't seem so scary anymore.

You're with the one who took care of you and taught you what you needed.

You dealt with the dragon and the mess it made.

You release your sadness and pain to it.

I cried and cried and cried.

I awoke the next day after the longest sleep of my life.

Soon, I would pack up my bags for college. I would travel again across the Clearing to another one far away.

I heard the campus was even wider and the sky bigger. I imagined it would be a whole new canvas, waiting for me to fill it up with my wildest dreams.

And maybe, who knows what will come true.

About the Authors

Joseph Legaspi was born in the Philippines and grew up in New York City. As a fiction writer, he has authored short stories, novels, and poems. His debut novel *A Three-Year Minute* has been ranked number four on Amazon's Best Seller List. Joseph has been a two-time finalist for the Storyshares 2021 and 2022 Story of the Year Contest for his respective works "Chance and Little Star" and "Hiding the Dragon." In nonfiction, he has worked as an essayist, columnist, and grant writer. His life work has also included teaching literacy and sharing his love of literature, for its unique way to inspire and move us all. He currently lives in New Jersey, USA.

Shekinah Oh and Tahlia Allen are contributing authors to the Storyshares library.

About the Publisher

Storyshares is a publisher focused on supporting the millions of teens and adults who struggle with reading by creating a new shelf in the library specifically for them. The ever-growing collection features content that is compelling and culturally relevant for teens and adults, yet still readable at a range of lower reading levels.

Storyshares generates content by engaging deeply with writers, bringing together a community to create this new kind of book. With more intriguing and approachable stories to choose from, the teens and adults who have fallen behind are improving their skills and beginning to discover the joy of reading.

For more information, visit storyshares.org.

Easy to Read. Hard to Put Down.